D1337359

DreamWorks

Spirit

RIDING FREE

❀ PALS · FOREVER ❀

EGMONT

We bring stories to life

First published in 2018 in the USA by Little, Brown and Company.
This edition published in Great Britain in 2020
by Egmont Books UK Ltd
2 Minster Court, 10th floor, London EC3R 7BB
www.egmontbooks.co.uk

ISBN 978 1 4052 9916 9
71167/001
Printed in the United Kingdom

Cover Design by Ching Chan

Egmont takes its responsibility to the planet
and it............................... from well-

DREAMWORKS
Spirit
RIDING FREE

PALs Forever

PALs

STACIA DEUTSCH

CHAPTER 1

'Miss Flores ... I mean, Mrs Prescott.' Snips raised his hand but didn't wait to be called on. 'Do you mean we have to do homework while we're on holiday?' He frowned. 'That wouldn't be fair.'

'Yes, Snips,' Mrs Prescott said.

Her new wedding ring glistened in the sunlight streaming in from the window. Lucky saw the metal glimmer and blinked hard. It was tough getting used to the idea that her teacher was now also her stepmum. But not as tough as the idea that they had a homework project over half term. She agreed with Snips. It wasn't fair.

'You don't have to do anything special for

1

this project,' Mrs Prescott explained.

'Just have a normal, fun half term. But I don't want your minds to be idle, so be prepared to share what you did with the class.'

A loud groan echoed through the room. It came from pretty much everyone, except Maricela.

She raised her hand but, unlike Snips, waited to be called on.

'I will recite a speech,' Maricela announced. 'Would twenty pages be too many?' She smiled. 'I have many important plans for the week. I'll be working at my father's office.' And then, as if no one knew who he was, she announced, 'He's the mayor.'

Mrs Prescott nodded slowly. 'We all know your father, Maricela, and that sounds like a very interesting half term.' She considered the project. 'Let's do this ... the presentation doesn't need to be a speech. It can be anything you want it to be.'

Maricela's hand went right back up. When she was called on, she asked, 'But it could be a speech if someone wanted, right?'

'Of course, but a short speech,' replied Mrs Prescott.

Pru leaned in so Lucky and Abigail could hear her whisper. 'Maricela wouldn't know a short speech if it hit her in the –'

'Pru,' Mrs Prescott interrupted. 'Why don't you share your idea for the presentation with the class?'

Pru snapped back up in her seat. 'I don't know what I'll do yet,' she said. 'My plans are pretty boring. I'm going to spend the break with my parents, helping out around the range.' She looked over at Abigail. 'It's not as if I get to go visit my cousins or anything.'

'You could always come with Snips and

3

me,' Abigail said. She turned to Mrs Prescott and the rest of her class. 'We're going to visit our mum's sister's brother's brother's sister and her husband in Dakota Springs.'

Lucky frowned. 'Wouldn't that be your aunt and uncle?'

'Maybe,' Abigail said. 'Anyway, they have a daughter a little younger than me.'

'Your cousin?' Pru prompted.

'I suppose.' Abigail continued, undaunted in her storytelling, 'We haven't seen them in a couple of years. When we were little, my cousin Ariella and I used to get along pretty well. But her family is very fancy, and she and I are grown-up ladies now, so she's probably become fancy, too! Snips and I are going to dress in our best clothes and use our best manners to show her how much we've matured.'

Snips groaned loud and long. 'Pru, can I stay here and help at the barn? Señor Carrots and me are good helpers.'

'Señor Carrots and I,' Mrs Prescott corrected.

'What she said.' Snips pointed at their teacher. Then he put his palms together and begged, 'Please, Pru. We'll sleep in a stall. You won't even know we're there.'

Pru laughed and shook her head. 'Sorry, Snips. My dad was pretty clear that there's some sort of job I have to take care of.' She sighed. 'I wish Lucky and Abigail could stay, though.'

'Ugh,' Snips said, pulling at the collar of his shirt as if he were wearing a necktie. 'When I am fancied to death, you'll be sorry.' He gave a dramatic performance of gasping and choking before flopping to the floor in a motionless heap.

'No one ever died from being too fancy,' Abigail said, rolling her eyes at her brother's theatrics. She told Mrs Prescott, 'I've been taking manners classes from Lucky's aunt

5

Cora for weeks. I'm ready to use my skills in the wild.'

'That sounds like a lovely holiday,' said Mrs Prescott. 'I'm sure the class is excited to hear all about it.' She then went around the room and asked other students what they were doing over the holiday.

'I'm going to help build a barn,' Turo said with a shrug. 'Nothing too exciting.'

'We're going to do nothing,' Mary Pat said.

'Nothing,' her twin sister, Bianca, echoed. 'If you want to stay here in Miradero,' she told Snips, fluttering her eyelashes, 'we could spend the whole break together.'

'That would be fun!' Mary Pat said sarcastically.

'Ugh.' Snips groaned again, peeling himself off the floor and sitting back at his desk. 'I'll take my chances with the fancy cousins.'

'Well then, class.' Mrs Prescott began wrapping it up. School was over and the holidays were about to begin. 'When you get back, you can each show us what you did in a skit, a song' – she looked to Maricela – 'a short speech, or however you choose to present your –'

'You didn't ask Lucky,' Abigail blurted out, then slapped a hand over her own mouth. 'Oh dear, shouting in class without being called on isn't very fancy. Sorry, Mrs Prescott.' She shrugged. 'Lucky's aunt Cora would say holding my tongue is a growth area for me. She told me to concentrate really hard on not speaking until spoken to. Argh! I don't know how anyone holds their thoughts in their head for so long without exploding. It makes my brain hurt. But,' Abigail went on, 'Mrs Prescott, you didn't call on Lucky.'

'That's because we're going on holiday together,' Lucky explained. It still felt odd that it wouldn't be just her dad and her going on adventures anymore.

'Yes, we are,' Mrs Prescott said, coming to stand with Lucky. 'We're going out to Destiny Falls. It's a bigger city than Miradero.' She looked at Lucky and smiled. 'I have no doubt we'll have a great adventure – the three of us together.'

Even though she wouldn't see her friends for a whole week, Lucky was determined to have a good time. It would be exciting to see somewhere new ... right? Throwing a smile on her face to mirror her stepmum's, she agreed, 'Yep. It'll be great!'

'I'll see you all back here in a week,' said Mrs Prescott as the students stood to leave. 'And don't forget to do your homework!'

CHAPTER 2

'Hurry up, Lucky, we have a train to catch.'

Jim Prescott was gathering the suitcases in the front hall. Lucky's bag was a small duffel compared to Kate's enormous case.

'Is Kate taking everything she owns?' Lucky asked with a small laugh. At school, Mrs Prescott was "Mrs Prescott," but at home she was "Kate."

'Of course I am,' Kate replied, coming in through the parlour with a smile. 'I've never been to a city as big as Destiny Falls before.'

'Really? Never?' Lucky had a hard time believing that. The Prescotts had come to

Miradero from a very big city. How was it possible that Kate had never even *been* to a big city?

Kate shook her head. 'Never! I can't wait to explore. Lucky, you'll show me everything, won't you?'

'Sure.' Lucky had never been to Destiny Falls, but she knew there was a theatre and several shopping streets, instead of just the one street in Miradero. There were quite a few restaurants and plenty of riding trails she and Spirit could explore.

Just as she was thinking about him, Spirit neighed loudly from outside the front door.

'Thanks for letting Spirit come along,' Lucky said to her dad. 'He's so excited!'

Spirit had been standing outside the door for hours while they all packed and got ready. Lucky heard him paw the ground with his hoof. 'We're coming,' she called. 'Be patient.'

Spirit whinnied again. He'd waited this long; he could wait a few more minutes.

'I'll ride Spirit down to the station,' Lucky told her dad and Kate. 'I'll meet you and the car there so I can help unload' – she eyed Kate's case – 'that!' Glancing at Kate, she winked and asked, 'Are you certain we aren't moving to Destiny Falls?'

Her dad snorted with a heavy laugh, then said, 'Go on ahead, Lucky. Tell the conductor that we're on the way.'

'Can do!' Lucky said, leaving her small bag with the luggage. She pranced out the door and was about to climb on Spirit's back when Pru and Abigail came galloping into the yard. Pru was on Chica Linda and Abigail was riding Boomerang.

'We came to escort you to the train,' Abigail explained while Lucky climbed onto Spirit's bare back. 'I'm not going to my cousins' house until tomorrow.' She leaned back in her saddle. 'One more day to get my skills in order. Today, I have my last lesson with your aunt.' Aunt Cora was staying in Miradero.

'Will it be to practise chewing with your mouth closed?' Pru suggested.

'Or a review class on where your elbows go while you eat?' Lucky teased.

'*Not* on the table,' Abigail said in a voice that mimicked Aunt Cora's. But then in her own voice, she said, 'I can't figure out where to put my elbows if they aren't resting on the table! They get so tired.'

The girls all laughed.

'I think we're reviewing greetings today,' Abigail said, turning to Lucky. With a slight bow, she said, 'It's very pleasant to make your acquaintance.'

'Seems to me like you've got it!' Lucky said with a giggle.

The horses began trotting away from Lucky's house. 'I can't believe Abigail and I are going out on adventures and you're staying here,' Lucky said to Pru.

'Well, my dad says he has something big planned over break,' Pru told them. 'Maybe that'll make up for my staying here.'

'*Oooohhhh*, a surprise? I *love* surprises!' Abigail squealed, but then corrected herself. 'I mean, I don't *always* love surprises, like when Snips put a frog in my bed – that was a bad surprise – but I do love good surprises! Like cake! Cake is always a good surprise.'

'So you don't have a clue what it could be?' Lucky asked Pru. She loved mysteries and would have wanted to have helped Pru solve this one, if she wasn't leaving town.

'Nope,' Pru said, pulling back on Chica Linda's reins. 'But since it's my dad, I'm guessing it's something horse related, like building new fences for the field or maybe going on a long trail ride if I'm lucky.'

The horses slowed as they arrived at the station. Lucky climbed down from Spirit's back. She'd ride the train and he'd run along, taking his own journey to meet her in Destiny Falls.

'Well.' Abigail looked at the big black train as it spewed smoke from the tracks. 'I guess this is farewell.'

'Only for a week,' Lucky said.

'A week that'll feel like *forever*,' Abigail said with a sigh.

'*Hmmm.*' Lucky thought for a moment, and then she smiled widely. 'I have a great idea! We should write one another letters while we are gone!'

'Oh, I love that,' Pru agreed. 'We can tell one another everything about our holidays!'

'And then we can turn in the letters for Mrs Prescott's homework project!' Abigail suggested.

'That's a great idea, Abigail! I'll write one tonight,' Lucky said, 'and I'll send it right away so it's there when you arrive at your cousins'.'

'Then I'll write to Pru,' Abigail continued.

'And I'll write to Lucky,' Pru finished. 'And then we'll switch around.'

'I love it,' Abigail said. 'Almost as much as I love cake and Boomerang.' She paused. Leaning forward over her saddle, Abigail told her horse, 'You know I love you more than cake, though.'

'Lucky!' Her father was calling.

Lucky looked over to see her dad and Kate were already on the train. Their bags were stacked in the luggage carriage.

'First to arrive, last to board,' Lucky said with a shrug. She said a quick goodbye to her friends and hurried onto the train.

As the train pulled away from the station, Lucky leaned out the window and shouted to Pru and Abigail, 'Don't forget to write!' And then to Spirit, 'See you soon!'

The train chugged slowly towards Destiny Falls.

It was sunset when they finally arrived.

Lucky looked out at the town in the golden light and was amazed. It was so different from Miradero. There were paved roads, more horse-drawn carriages, and big, ornate buildings. A quick look at Kate confirmed that she was even more amazed than Lucky. Her eyes were wide and she craned her neck, trying to take everything in through the window.

'I have a surprise for you,' Mr Prescott said as the train gave its final chug.

'That's funny,' Lucky remarked. 'Pru's dad had a surprise for her, too. I wonder if there's a half term surprise waiting for Abigail.'

'I guess half term is just a perfect time for surprises,' Mr Prescott said with a smile.

'Well?' Lucky asked expectantly. 'What *is* the surprise? I can't wait to –'

'Hiya, RF!' An all-too-familiar voice floated through the door of their train compartment to interrupt Lucky. 'Welcome to Destiny Falls!'

'Oh, good grief,' Lucky muttered, sinking down in her seat. 'Why couldn't the surprise be ice cream or balloons or some top-grade oats for Spirit?' Any of those would have been better than a meet-up with her cousin Julian, who was now leaning against the compartment door and grinning at her. Julian was nothing but trouble, and he always called her *RF*. He thought it was funny because it was short for 'Rabbit's Foot,' as in lucky rabbit's feet.

Lucky sighed. So much for a relaxing holiday with her new family. With Julian around, she would have to watch her back at every turn. Who knew what kind of tricks he could get up to?

'Hello, Uncle Jim,' Julian said cheerfully. He helped unload their luggage and placed it in a cart that was far nicer than any cart in Miradero. He gave a bow and said, 'Aunt Kate. It's nice to see you again.' Lucky's dad and stepmum both smiled and greeted him politely.

Lucky couldn't help thinking that Abigail could have taken greeting lessons from Julian instead of Aunt Cora. He was smooth and savvy. Of course, she hoped her dad still had his wallet after the big hug Julian gave him. Julian turned to Lucky with a grin.

'Hi.' Lucky took a deep breath and promised herself that having Julian around would in no way diminish her excitement about the holiday. 'It's interesting to find you here,' Lucky said. 'What are you doing in Destiny Falls?'

'My parents are building a new train depot and helping this place become an even bigger city,' Julian explained as he pushed the luggage cart and led them off the train. 'Just like when you moved to Miradero to get things settled, my family moved here.' He gave her a nudge. 'I just know that your dad is going to love the place. Wait until he sees the plans for the new station. He's going to want to get started building it right away.'

Lucky looked around at the small but clean and pretty station they were in. There was art on the walls and ornate iron benches to sit on while waiting. That was already more than they had at home. 'Looks fine to me,' Lucky said as they made their way to the exit and the street beyond.

'It's going to be incredible!' Julian said. He held out his hand to help Lucky into the carriage that was waiting for them. 'There will be a restaurant and a boot shine and a place to store your luggage if you're just here touring the city for the day.' He grinned. 'And then, there will be all the new train lines to cities all over the frontier. This city is going to be the centre of the region!' He seemed so excited about the changes, but Lucky wanted to think about what they were seeing today, not what the city might be like in the future. Who even knew when she'd be back here?

'I'll ride Spirit, if that's OK,' she said, refusing Julian's hand. 'Can I, Dad?'

'Of course,' her father said. 'Just follow us so you don't get lost.'

Lucky climbed onto Spirit's back and they settled in at a slow pace behind the wagon. She saw her father sit back in the plush velvet seats, wrapping his arm around Kate. Julian sat on the front bench with the driver.

'Spirit,' Lucky said, leaning forward and wrapping her arms around her horse's neck. 'The best thing about a big city is that you don't have to see everyone all the time. There will be so many places to go, people to see, adventures to have. We can see Julian when we want and get lost in the crowds when we want, too.' She sat up and let the last few rays of sunshine warm her face. 'This is going to be the best holiday. I just know it!'

Dear Abigail,

Greetings from Destiny Falls! We just got here a little while ago, and you are not going to believe who was waiting at the station. It was Julian!

His family is living in Destiny Falls to help set up the new train depot. He's acting as smug as ever. I'll need to watch him with eagle eyes in case he tries to be tricky again!

When Julian told us about the new train station, I got really worried my dad was going to work this whole holiday, but he promised he'd have time for me. We are going to take a horse ride tomorrow. Just us. I can't wait to see the town in the daylight.

You'd be so impressed. The hotel we

are staying at is <u>huge</u>. It's five storeys, and there's a café on the first floor that has the biggest, most delicious banana splits I have ever eaten. I couldn't even finish mine!

Kate told me she heard the schoolhouse here is as if three of our schools were put together, and — get this — there are even separate classrooms for different grade levels! No, I am not kidding. Could you imagine if Snips were in a different class than ours? I think that would be a great idea.

Shopping is how I remember from living in the city. There isn't just one supermarket for most things. Dad promised we'd go to a hat shop for hats, a dress shop for dresses (well ... maybe more than one dress shop ...),

and even a men's shop for my dad
to buy a suit.

I can't wait to see it all. The
adventure starts at sunrise! I also
can't wait until you write to me.

PALs forever,

Lucky ☆

PS: I hope Julian doesn't think
I'm hanging out with him. We are <u>not</u>
hanging out. No way. Never. Nuh-uh.
Negative. No.

CHAPTER 3

'Pru!'

Day one of the holidays and Pru was already working at the barn. She'd just left Lucky at the train station, and Abigail had gone home to pack her bags.

Pru sighed. 'Be right there,' she called out to her father. First she had to make sure that Chica Linda had enough hay and fresh water.

'It's just going to be you and me for a while,' she told her horse. Pru gave Chica Linda a scratch behind the ears. 'Spirit is off with Lucky, and Boomerang is going tomorrow with Abigail. Even Señor Carrots will be gone the whole half term.' Chica

Linda whinnied. 'The good news is that Dad said he has something planned,' Pru told Chica Linda as she loaded more hay into the stall. 'Whatever it is, I hope it'll be fun,' Pru said, then rushed out of the barn to find her dad.

He was sitting on a bale of hay by the corral. There was a clipboard in his hand, and he was making notes on a sheet of paper.

'I've made a list of all the things you need to do in the next few days,' he said. With a flick of his wrist, he turned the paper towards her, and Pru read the list out loud.

'Mend fences, paint barn, muck stalls, spread manure ... ' OK, that one was her least favourite, but it had to be done. These were normal things and exactly what Pru assumed she'd be doing her entire break from school. Adventures with Chica Linda would have to wait until the workday was done.

There were more items on her dad's list, so Pru read on. 'Put up posters, assign activities, get barrels from Turo, order ice cream from Mr Winthrop, buy blue ribbons at the supermarket ... Uh, Dad?' Pru was confused about the last few items. 'These other things are strange. What's going on?'

'I told you I had something big planned for this week, Pru,' her father said. 'A children's rodeo!' He turned the list back around and jotted *Set up lunch tables* onto it. And under that, *Order lunches*.

'A rodeo?' Pru squinted in the afternoon sunlight. 'Oh. I figured we would be building fences for the field or maybe taking a ride up to Patriot's Peak.' She'd always wanted to go there but had never had the chance.

'Well, I hope you're not too let down. This children's rodeo is going to be a lot of work. I was thinking with your time off from school, you could lend me a hand.' Mr Granger sighed and tapped his pen on his clipboard. 'I know I'm forgetting things, and I haven't even begun to prepare for the Wranglers' meeting.' He turned to a blank page and wrote *Meeting stuff* at the top of the paper. Then, he set down the pen. 'Will you be able to help?'

'Of course,' Pru answered.

Her dad ran his hands over his face. 'Boy, am I glad to hear that. The Frontier Wranglers' Association's annual meeting was moved to Miradero last minute. Obviously I'm thrilled at the opportunity, but there's so much to be done. Twenty wranglers and their families are coming. The meeting is a no-brainer, but it's a tradition to hold a rodeo to entertain the kids, and I have no idea where to start.' He frowned.

'So,' Pru said slowly, 'if twenty wranglers

are coming, how many kids does that mean for the children's rodeo?'

'Eight to ten,' Mr Granger said. 'Maybe a few more. I'm not sure.'

'What exactly do you need me to do?' Pru asked.

'Well,' Mr Granger said, 'I was thinking that while I take care of the meeting and the wranglers, it might be fun for you to organise and run the rodeo by yourself. I'm sure you could handle it on your own, and it'd sure be a big help to me.'

'Run the rodeo?' That sounded ... amazing! Pru, Lucky and Abigail had run a summer camp before, so Pru knew everything she had to do to entertain kids and keep them busy. Her father's list was a good place to start, but there were going to be so many other things that she'd need to prepare.

Pru wished that Lucky and Abigail were there to help. It was a little scary having to do all the preparation for a rodeo *and* host it on her own. It would be only eight or ten kids, but still, rowdy frontier kids needed more than a babysitter – Pru was determined to do the job and to do it well.

'I'll take care of it, Dad,' she said, taking the clipboard and pen, then handing her dad the page on which he'd written *Meeting stuff*. 'You just worry about planning the meeting, OK?'

'Are you sure?' Mr Granger said.

'Yup!' Pru said with a grin. 'Leave the rodeo to me.'

'All righty, then,' Mr Granger said, standing up and dusting the hay from his trousers. 'I trust you to do a good job, Pru.'

'I will,' she said, then took the list with her into the barn. She posted the clipboard on a nail near the barn door. 'Check it out,

Chica Linda,' she gushed. 'Great news. We're organising a kids' rodeo!'

The horse answered with a loud neigh.

Pru studied the list. She needed to do all those things, plus make sure there were good, clean stalls for the rodeo kids to leave their horses, room to store their tack, enough hay and water and feed and – *wow*. It felt a little overwhelming.

'Hiya, Pru.' Pru turned to see Turo entering the barn.

'Hi, Turo!' Pru said. 'What's going on?'

'I'm going to be heading to my cousin's place to help with the barn, and I was wondering if I could borrow a duffel bag. I can't find mine.'

'Sure.' As Pru headed to the tack room to grab one, she remembered her father had written Turo's name on their list of things to do. *Get barrels from Turo.* When she handed

Turo her duffel, she said, 'Do you happen to have extra barrels lying around?'

'Barrels?' Turo asked. 'What for?'

'It turns out that the big plan my dad has over break is to organise a children's rodeo, and he asked me to take care of it!' Pru smiled. 'The barrels would be awesome for barrel racing!'

Turo frowned. 'Unfortunately, I only make them when people need them.'

'Oh.' Pru bit her lip. 'So you don't have any right now?'

'No,' Turo said, shaking his head. 'No barrels.'

'And you wouldn't be able to make a few real quick?' Pru prodded.

'I'm sorry, Pru, but that's an all-day job.'

'Oh.' Pru deflated slightly. 'Well, that's OK. I'll figure something out.'

'Are you sure?' Turo asked. 'I could maybe

32

put off going to my cousin's to build some barrels for you. Putting on a rodeo is a lot of work; I'm sure you need the help.'

'No,' Pru said firmly. 'I'll take care of it. It'll be fine – I know it.'

'OK.' Turo shrugged. He took the duffel bag from her. 'If you're positive. I can't wait to hear how it goes!' He waved and headed out of the barn. 'See ya!'

'Yeah. See ya,' Pru echoed, feeling slightly uncertain. She could do this by herself ... couldn't she? She took down the clipboard from the wall and found a spot to sit in Chica Linda's stall.

'I've got this,' she told herself, letting the negative feelings pass. 'So no barrel racing. What other events should we do, Chica Linda?'

The horse was silent.

Pru closed her eyes, trying to think of

what they'd done at the hundreds of rodeos she'd gone to, but nothing came to mind. Pru knew she was trying too hard.

Deciding to think about it later, she turned to a new piece of paper and took out the pen. She was going to write a letter to Lucky.

Dear Lucky,

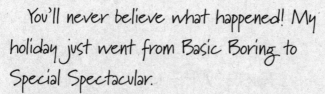

You'll never believe what happened! My holiday just went from Basic Boring to Special Spectacular.

Apparently, we're going to be hosting the Frontier Wranglers' Association's annual meeting. That means wranglers and their kids are coming to Miradero this weekend, and <u>that</u> means the kids will have their traditional children's rodeo this weekend. The spectacular part is that my dad wants <u>me</u> to organise the rodeo while he organises the meeting!

I wish you and Abigail were here to do it with me. It's gonna be a lot of work, but everyone knows that I love rodeos! I can't wait to show my dad that I can do it by myself.

Unfortunately, I've already met a bit of a hurdle. With Turo going out of town, it turns out that there aren't any barrels available for a barrel race. And what's a rodeo without a barrel race? I'm gonna have to be creative and figure out something else I can do. I'll just have to be imaginative like you always are and brainstorm like Abigail always does.

Right now, I'm trying to make a list of rodeo events. ... ~~We~~ I mean, I could make three days out of the rodeo: one will be for speed, one will be for skills, and one will be just for fun.

So on speed day, the kids could do racing and jumping (but no barrel races).

On skills day, they'll do pole bending, scarecrow roping, and maybe some other kinds of tricks.

Finally, on fun day, we can do egg-in-spoon races, a Boot Scoot, and some horse painting!

Hey, thanks! Before I wrote to you, I was having trouble coming up with stuff to do, and now I have a whole list! See, you can help all the way from Destiny Falls.

This rodeo is going to be so much fun! I'll make sure of it, even without Turo's barrels. If you have any more good ideas, let me know!

Hope you are having a good time
with your dad and our teacher.

PALs forever,

Pru

CHAPTER 4

'Aunt Karen! Uncle Tony! Ariella!'
Abigail leaped off Boomerang's back
and rushed to greet her family. As she was
running, she caught herself and remembered
that 'ladies don't run.' Instead, she smoothed
her nicest pair of riding trousers, straightened
her best button-down top, and walked
carefully towards her relatives. They were
standing on the steps of a big yellow house
with a long wraparound porch that housed a
small dining table and chairs.

Aunt Karen was her mum's sister and it
had been a while since they'd all seen one
another.

Snips tumbled off Señor Carrots's back and

sauntered slowly to the house as well. Abigail glanced at him, noted that he had a streak of dirt across his forehead, and inwardly groaned. She then looked at the small girl standing on the steps. Though Ariella was ten, the age right between Snips and Abigail, she was short for her age and had dark-brown hair neatly braided down her back. Eyeing her outfit, Abigail noted that Ariella wasn't *dressed* very fancy – she dressed how the other girls in Miradero did – but that didn't mean she didn't *act* fancy.

But when she and Snips got closer, Ariella took one look at Abigail and her perfectly primed outfit and instead turned towards Snips.

'Hey,' she said to him.

'Hey,' he replied.

'Nice donkey,' she said with a grin.

'Thanks,' Snips said.

Abigail noticed right away that she complimented Señor Carrots but not Boomerang, who was far more majestic than the little donkey. Boomerang snorted at the offence.

Snips said, 'Me and Señor Carrots are hungry after the long ride. Got any snacks?'

'Snips!' Abigail hissed under her breath. 'Polite people don't beg for food.' That was one of the things Lucky's aunt Cora had taught her. 'Wait until snacks are offered.'

'But we're hungry,' Snips whispered back.

'That's all right, dear,' Aunt Karen said, motioning back to the table on the porch. 'We expected that you'd be famished after the long ride. Our cook is serving lunch as we speak.'

Abigail looked to the table, where an aubergine-shaped man in a white shirt was setting out plates. She inhaled deeply.

Whatever he was serving smelled delicious. She was hungry, too, but wasn't going to blurt it out like her brother. Instead, Abigail said, 'That sounds lovely. I can't wait to partake in a meal.' Perhaps she should have said, *I look forward to partaking* ... She couldn't remember the correct grammar. It was too late now.

'Come along,' Uncle Tony said, taking their packs off Boomerang and handing them to a woman who had appeared so quietly that Abigail hadn't even noticed her. 'Martha will set these in your rooms.'

'Rooms?' Snips asked. 'I have my own room?'

'Of course!' Aunt Karen said, tossing back her light-coloured hair with a laugh. 'You'll be in the spare room near Ariella, while Abigail here will be in the guest room next to Ashton.'

'Oh, the baby!' Abigail gushed. 'I can't wait

to meet him.' Ashton was a toddler now. Abigail had last visited right before he was born. That was the last time they'd all been together.

'He's not such a baby anymore,' Aunt Karen said.

'More of a terror,' Uncle Tony remarked.

I have a brother like that, too, Abigail thought. With the similarities between their brothers, Abigail hoped that Ariella would be similar to her.

'Ashton is napping now,' Aunt Karen said. 'So let's enjoy lunch while we can.'

They went to the porch and sat down.

Chef Paul filled their plates with chicken and rice. While Abigail was trying to recall which fork to use, the smaller one or the bigger one, Snips picked up a chicken leg with his fingers and took a huge bite, juices dripping down his chin. He wiped his mouth on his sleeve.

'Yum,' he said.

'Snips!' Abigail hissed. She'd have to talk to him in private later.

After a moment's hesitation, Abigail noticed that her uncle picked up the bigger fork, so she did the same. She used her knife, as she'd been taught, and sliced a small piece of meat. Chew. Swallow. Then, after checking her elbows were not on the table, she started to cut another piece.

'I have the best plans for this week!' Ariella announced in an excited whisper so her parents couldn't hear. 'There's a huge surprise, and I want you to be part of it!' Abigail noticed that Ariella hadn't started eating yet and wondered if this was one of those situations where you were supposed to wait for others to start. Manners were confusing.

'I love surprises!' Snips roared through a

mouthful of rice. Speckles of his food sprayed across the table and hit Abigail in the eye.

'*Eww,*' she said, gently dabbing at her eyelid with her crisp linen napkin. 'I enjoy an unexpected occurrence as well,' she said, while dipping her fork into the rice and collecting a few grains, then placing them carefully in her mouth. Chew. Swallow.

At this rate, Abigail figured she'd be done eating the meal in two or three years.

'What's the surprise?' Snips asked.

Ariella glanced at her parents, who were still talking to each other and not listening to them. 'I can't tell you. But it's big!'

'*Ooohh,*' Snips said. 'Can Señor Carrots help, too? He loves to help.'

Ariella nodded. 'We'll find just the right job for your magnificent steed.'

'What about Boomerang?' Abigail asked hesitantly. 'He loves helping, too.'

Ariella looked across the yard to where Boomerang was walking in circles around a tree. There was a low branch and he hit his head on it, then shook off the bump, continuing around. On the next revolution, he hit his head again, as if this were the first time he'd seen the branch. And so on ... again and again.

'Maybe. We'll see,' Ariella said, before turning away.

What?! Boomerang, though a little mixed up, was a much finer 'steed' than Snips's donkey. Abigail felt as if something was off, and she wanted to make it right.

'Since the surprise is a secret,' Abigail said, 'let's talk about the other things we are going to do. I can't wait to explore the house and the garden. Are there good trails to ride around here?'

Ariella snorted and said under her breath, 'Exploring is boring.'

Abigail wasn't sure she'd heard her cousin right. She remembered Ariella being a lot of fun. They'd had a blast when they were together before; they had played hide-and-seek in the big house and had nighttime bonfires. The house had a beautiful stable and Abigail remembered building a maze out of hay bales with Ariella and sneaking out at night to ride horses in the ring. None of that seemed boring then. But maybe Ariella was too fancy for outdoor activities now.

Aunt Karen faced the children and said, 'After lunch, you and Snips can rest a bit, and then we will all go to the stables together. I'd love to take you on a ride down to the lake where you can swim.'

Abigail thought it sounded fun until

Ariella rolled her eyes and said, 'Yeah, sure,' as if it were the worst plan ever.

Aunt Karen glanced at Uncle Tony and sighed.

Uncle Tony sighed back at her, then said cheerily, 'I'll hook up the little cart and Ashton can come along.'

'It'll be a fine adventure,' Aunt Karen said. 'Our first one of the week.'

'Let's finish lunch so we can get started,' Uncle Tony said, digging back into his meal with the appropriate fork.

Abigail continued to work at her food but was getting impatient. It would have been easier to eat like Snips, but Abigail was prepared for a fancy holiday, and she wasn't going to mess it up.

'I'm done,' Ariella announced, pushing back from the table.

'Huh?' Abigail looked up from her food to discover that her cousin had eaten everything on her plate without lifting a piece of silverware. There were chicken bits all over her hands and rice stuck in her fingernails. Her dress had grease stains, similar to the stains on Snips's fine shirt.

It was as if her aunt and uncle didn't notice what was going on at the table. They were so deep in conversation again that when Ariella grabbed a cookie off the dessert tray and told Snips, 'Come on. Let's get out of here,' they didn't say anything.

Abigail rose to join her cousin and her brother, when her aunt realised what was going on.

'Stay,' she told Abigail. 'Let the little kids run off. You can enjoy your dessert in peace with your uncle and me. We'd love to hear all about Miradero.' Abigail sat back down in her chair and watched as Snips and Ariella ran towards the barn, hand in hand, laughing.

'How is my dear sister?' Aunt Karen asked.

Abigail took a tiny bite of her cookie. Chewed. Swallowed. Dabbed her lips with her napkin, then replied, 'She's doing well.'

Dear Pru,

Things are good at my cousins'
house, but they're really strange.
Ariella is not at all how I
remember her. I don't like even
thinking this, but I get the feeling
she's more interested in hanging out
with Snips than with me.
   That's crazy! Right? I know.
   I must be imagining things.
   I'll just have to try harder to
show her that I fit in here at the
fancy house with their fancy chef and
fancy barn and fancy life. It'll take
a little more effort, but she'll notice
how much I belong and will stop
hanging out so much with Snips, who
isn't trying at all. The more fancy

I am, the more not-fancy Snips
will look. There's no way my cousin
could like _not-fancy_ better than
fancy. I mean, you should see this
place! She has the ultimate fancy
life!

You can't run in the halls or
wear shoes on the carpets. There's
no food allowed anywhere except
at the dining table ... and there
are four tables to choose from! Not
even counting the one outside on
the porch.

In the barn, we don't do
any of the work because there
are groomsmen to saddle and
unsaddle the horses. Boomerang
is so spoiled. He's getting bathed

every day, and I haven't even braided his mane because the professionals keep doing it before I get there. All I have to do is show up if I want to ride. The men at the barn even boost me into the saddle and help me down ... which is a little weird, but since it's fancy, and I'm all about fancy living nowadays, I let them.

There's going to be a big surprise that Ariella keeps talking about, but she refuses to let us in on it. With how fancy my aunt and uncle are, I'm guessing that it is a fine night out at the opera or perhaps a carriage ride through the park. Oh, I know! Maybe it's a ball!

That would be the best thing ever!
I really hope the surprise is a ball.
I brought the perfect dress for a
night of dancing. I bet they will
have little sandwiches and we can
all drink tea from porcelain cups.

I've learned all these good
manners and have been using
them as best as I can, but a ball
would be the greatest place to
show off what Cora taught me. I
would curtsy and bow. I could eat
politely and show off my brand-
new waltzing skills.

I am going to impress Ariella
so much that she will invite me back
next half term. Not Snips, who ate
with his fingers, spilled juice on an

expensive rug, broke an antique vase and brought Señor Carrots into the kitchen for a late-night snack.

In the competition of fancy versus not-fancy, I will be the winner.

Wish me luck.

PALs forever,

Abigail

CHAPTER 5

'Isn't Destiny Falls fabulous?' Julian asked for the tenth time in ten minutes.

Lucky's day was *not* turning out how she'd expected. Her dad had promised a great day, just the two of them, but instead had somehow gotten roped into attending a meeting about the railroad station. To make it up to her, Lucky's dad said he'd meet up for a late lunch and take her out then. Kate was planning to attend an all-day painting class at the local art shop, so that left Lucky with Julian to take a tour of the town.

Lucky wished she'd gone with Kate to the painting class instead.

'It's fabulous for sure,' Lucky repeated for

the tenth time. She actually really did like the town but felt reluctant to let Julian know that, since he was so enthusiastic about everything.

In fact, Lucky was suspicious. Why *was* Julian so enthusiastic about Destiny Falls?

'Let's see the school,' Julian said, leading her down a side street from the main square. 'And afterwards, I'll show you the best barn in town. You and Spirit are going to love it. It's so much better than Pru's little place.'

'The Granger stable is amazing.' Lucky felt defensive. 'It has just the right number of stalls, and the riding ring and turnouts are great. Spirit is perfectly happy there.'

'Yeah, well, I'll bet that Spirit likes this barn better,' Julian said, putting out his hand to shake. 'A pound?'

'Sure,' Lucky said, shaking his hand. 'Easy money.'

'We'll see what Spirit says,' Julian told Lucky.

Spirit neighed. He'd met Lucky in the town square. Julian was already on his horse, ready to ride to the school.

Lucky jumped on Spirit's back. 'I thought Kate wanted to see the school, too,' Lucky said. 'Should we wait for her and do it later?'

'She'll see the school,' Julian said. 'Aunt Kate has a meeting with the principal tomorrow.'

'First, it's weird to hear you call her 'aunt,' and second, why would she meet the principal?' Lucky didn't understand. There was no reason to meet the boss of the school, unless ... But that wasn't possible ... Then again, Kate *did* bring everything she owned to Destiny Falls ...

Julian had also said that once her dad saw

the plans for the new train station, he would want to 'get started' ...

As Lucky began connecting the dots, her mind started racing faster and faster. She felt almost dizzy from her conclusion. She shook it off and leaned over Spirit's neck. 'We're only here for a week, boy. Not forever.' She wasn't sure if she was trying to reassure him or herself.

Spirit bobbed his head comfortingly.

As much as Lucky hated to admit it, the school really was amazing. It was big and had a gymnasium for sporting events.

All the kids were organised into sports teams. Different *kinds* of teams for different sports, too! And there was even a small theatre with a stage for school plays.

Lucky couldn't help thinking how Maricela would look at the centre of the stage, with a spotlight right on her. Too bad Maricela didn't want to move to Destiny Falls with … No, wait, she was thinking about moving again. Lucky stamped that thought out of her head and climbed on Spirit's back to follow Julian to the local barn.

'See? Everything is modern and new here,' Julian was saying. 'And now, I'm going to earn that pound.' He looked to Spirit. 'Hey, horse, check out the field.'

Lucky followed Julian's gaze to a large area behind the multi-stall barn structure. There was a huge open field with maybe twenty horses milling around, eating the grass and hanging out together.

'It's completely open,' Julian said. 'They don't even bother with fences or gates because the horses don't want to leave.'

One of the problems at the Grangers' barn was that Spirit hated being locked inside.

But it was definitely safer to have the horses shut in for the night, and Lucky had already had issues with horse rustlers who wanted to 'steal' Spirit away.

'Never any problems here,' Julian assured Lucky, as if reading her thoughts. 'Everyone respects one another's horses, and all the horses are treated equally.'

Spirit whinnied and Lucky said, 'You really want to go check it out? Are you sure?'

Spirit whinnied again, and Lucky climbed down. 'It's not the wild,' she warned him. 'You don't have to like it.' She noticed a stream ran through the grass with shady trees lining the sides of the water. The horses all looked happy.

Julian dismounted as well, but his horse stuck around while Spirit went to meet the Destiny Falls herd.

'You owe me a pound,' Julian said, holding out his palm. 'Want to go two for nothing?'

Spirit trotted around the field happily. 'Fine,' Lucky grunted. 'What are you going to bet me now?'

'That you'll want to see a play tonight.' He held up two tickets for a new musical. 'Everyone loves the railroad here, and my family gets free stuff all the time because of it.'

'Those tickets were free?' Lucky couldn't believe it. 'No one gives us free stuff in Miradero.'

Julian waved the tickets in front of her impatiently. 'So, do you want to go? You'll be treated like royalty, and we can even go backstage afterwards to meet the actors.'

Oh, she really did want to go. Julian definitely knew exactly how to push her buttons, but she never got to go see plays in Miradero, and she had *never* been able to go backstage!

Lucky sighed. 'OK. You win that bet, too.'

Lucky dug two pounds out of her boot and handed them to him. 'I don't really want to go with *you*, but I do want to go.'

'I just love spending your money,' Julian said, putting the coins in his pocket. He looked around with a grin. 'Now, what else can I bet you?'

'You aren't getting any more of my money,' Lucky said. She whistled for Spirit. 'I think Spirit and I should tour around by ourselves now,' she told her cousin. 'I'll go find my dad. Maybe he's ready for lunch.'

'He's not ready,' Julian insisted. 'There's a lot to be done here, and everyone is depending on Uncle Jim.'

The way he said it raised Lucky's suspicions again.

'Want to see a nice new house?' Julian asked. 'It's for sale.'

'Why would I want to do that?!' Lucky

demanded as she settled on Spirit's back. She pulled his mane a bit too tightly and Spirit shook her hand loose. 'I already have a house!'

'I'll bet you a pound that you'll like this house better than the one you have in Miradero,' Julian said. 'It's next door to my new house.' He grinned again.

'I'm not taking the bet!' Lucky shouted. 'I don't want to see any new houses. And I don't want to *ever* live next door to you.' She was angry and could feel her heart racing. 'No matter what you think is happening here, my family is *not* moving to Destiny Falls!' She squeezed Spirit's flanks and nudged him into a gallop, leaving Julian behind.

His words echoed in the back of her mind all the way to town.

Lucky found her dad sitting in the hotel restaurant. He was surrounded by men who worked at the railroad. They were all wearing suits and ties.

'Dad!' She rushed into the restaurant, pushing past a waiter to reach the table.

'Lucky?' Jim stood and asked, 'What are you doing here? Where's Julian?' He glanced over her shoulder expectantly.

'I left him at the stables because he wanted to show me the house next to his,' Lucky said. 'He's acting like –'

'Oh, that Julian,' Jim said with a light laugh. 'He sure can get under your skin.' He looked at the other men at the table politely. 'Please excuse us for a moment.' Jim pulled Lucky to a more private area.

As soon as they were alone, Jim frowned slightly. 'Lucky, you know better. You can't just barge in here like that. This is an important meeting about the new railroad station.'

'I –' Lucky began, but her father interrupted.

'Things are going so well. Don't you just love it here? It's so bustling and exciting. There's always something going on,' he said.

'Unfortunately, I'm going to have to cancel our lunch, but I should have this all wrapped up by dinner. You, Kate and I can all go out to celebrate.'

'I might be going to the theatre with Julian,' Lucky said glumly. She didn't know if that was still happening. Or if she even wanted to go.

'Terrific!' Jim replied. 'Then I'll celebrate with Kate. We'll have a date!'

'*Ugh,*' Lucky moaned. This was supposed to be her special day with her dad. Not Kate's date night. And certainly not a special day for the men waiting patiently at the dining table. 'Dad, I need to ask –'

Jim put up a hand. 'Later, Lucky. I need to get back to the meeting.' Something by the restaurant doorway caught his eye. Lucky turned her head. It was Julian, standing there, smiling and waving as if nothing had happened between them. 'Go on with Julian to see that house,' her father said. 'He told me he was going to introduce you to some of the kids in town. It'll be good for you to make new friends.'

'But I like my old friends!' Lucky cried.

Jim put his arm around her shoulder and escorted Lucky towards Julian. 'A young girl can never have too many friends,' he said. 'Hello, Julian. Lucky is looking forward to the rest of the tour and the show this evening. Thank you for entertaining her.'

Lucky felt sick as Julian gave a small bow and said, 'It's my pleasure.' Catching Lucky's eye, he winked.

Maybe someday Lucky should have a heart-to-heart about Julian with her dad. But obviously that day wouldn't be today.

'Dad?' Lucky said before they left the restaurant. 'Can I borrow five pounds?'

'That's a lot of money,' Jim said, fishing

out his wallet. 'What do you need it for?'

'I don't know,' Lucky said. 'But I'm betting the money will come in handy.'

'It's always good to be prepared,' Julian chirped.

When Jim walked away, Lucky turned to Julian. 'I bet you a pound you can't make me like Destiny Falls enough to want to live here.' She tucked the money her father gave her into her boot and stomped away.

'You're on,' Julian called out, chasing after her. 'I'm always game for a challenge.'

Dear Pru,

I think something terrible is happening. I haven't been able to talk to my dad about it yet because I can't seem to get him alone, but ... I think we're moving to Destiny Falls! Julian has been showing me around the town all day, and he keeps saying how much I'd like the school and how much Spirit will like the stables and how the house right next to his is for sale. Julian certainly seems sure that we're moving, and I can't help thinking he's right!

Julian and I went to see a show tonight. The play itself was amazing. There were bright lights and really beautiful costumes, and the story was about a group of three friends — just like us! It would've been a night out of a dream, except for the sound of Julian crunching on popcorn next to me the entire time. Afterwards, my dad was supposed to meet us at the ice cream parlour. I was going to try again to talk to him about the move, but he never showed up!

Apparently, he didn't make his dinner date with Kate, either. My dad was still at a meeting with the railroad people until late, and when I got home, Kate was asleep. So I just went to sleep, too. He must have been out most of the night.

I know, I know. I shouldn't jump to conclusions without asking someone about it, but it's as if Dad and Kate aren't even on this holiday with me! Here, let me tell you what I know. I'm sure if you reason it out how Boxcar Bonnie does, you'll agree that all signs point to us moving to Destiny Falls.

1. Julian showed Spirit the amazing local barn and bet me how much Spirit would like it. (It is really nice but definitely not as nice as yours.)

2. Dad told Julian to introduce me to people so I could make new friends. (He said — actually said — it would be good for me to make new friends, as if I needed to replace the friends I already have!)

3. Kate is meeting with the school principal today. (Why would she need to meet with the principal here unless it was for a job?)

4. Kate brought pretty much everything she owned on this holiday. (I wish I'd never joked about us moving here.)

5. The house next to Julian's is for sale, and my dad told me to go see it with him. (Why would I need to go see some silly house?!)

6. My dad is in important meetings all day every day. (It's like they can't make any decisions without him!)

7. Dad keeps asking if I like it here. (As if he really cares!)

That's seven clues. That's more clues than even Boxcar Bonnie ever uses.

She only needs three or four clues, and then she's certain enough to solve the mystery. I don't need to talk to my dad anymore because my clues can only point to one thing:

We're moving to Destiny Falls.

Pru! Help! I need to do something before everything gets settled!

I need to convince my dad that we <u>can't</u> — just <u>CAN'T</u> — move away from Miradero, but I'm not going to be able to do it alone. I need you and Abigail to drop what you're doing and come here <u>right now</u> to help me convince my dad not to make us move so no one buys a new house or gets a new job or anything like that! I know you have the rodeo and that Abigail is having fun with her family, but you need to go get her and then hurry to Destiny Falls — before it's too late.

PALs forever?

Lucky ☆

CHAPTER 6

'I need ten silver trophies,' Pru told the new manager at the Miradero Supermarket. She'd spent the last couple of days cleaning the barn and getting the arena ready for the rodeo. The wranglers and their kids were coming the very next day. It was time to get all the rodeo supplies!

'I only have one,' the manager replied with a shrug. 'And it's gold.' He showed her the price for the gold cup on a thick wooden base.

'Oh, that's way over my budget,' Pru said, frowning. 'OK, how about ribbons? I can mix up first place blue ones with some white ones for participation.'

'No ribbons,' the man said. He was tall and thin and was wearing a brown apron. Pru was sure that Abigail would say that he looked like a pencil. The thought made her chuckle.

'Is it funny that I don't have ribbons?' the man asked, misunderstanding why she'd chuckled.

Pru immediately clammed up. 'No,' she said quickly. 'It's actually kind of disappointing.'

'Can I help you with something else?' He looked around the shop as if he were very busy and she were wasting his time, even though there were no other customers.

Pru scratched her head. 'I'm not sure what to do about the trophies. How about hot dogs and buns? I need ten, wait, no ... ' She still wasn't one hundred percent sure how many kids there would be, but they would need to eat, and some kids might want two hot dogs, so she said, 'Twenty. I need twenty hot dogs and buns.'

'I have the hot dogs but no buns,' the man told her. 'They'll be in on Friday.'

'I need them tomorrow,' Pru said. She actually needed lunch for three days, but hot dogs were on her plan for day one. That plan was going to change. 'How about sandwich bread and deli meat?'

'Meat, yes,' the man answered. 'Bread, no.'

'Friday?' Pru asked, getting a vibe on the situation.

'Bakery ran out of flour, and their shipment hasn't arrived,' he explained. Then he looked at the shop door as if someone were coming in, but no one was there.

'What else can I make for the kids for lunch that doesn't involve bread?' Pru wondered out loud.

'Salad,' the man offered. 'We have a lot of lettuce.'

'Argh.' Though Pru liked salad, it wasn't a very good choice for the kids at the rodeo.

'Let me think about it,' she said, reviewing her list in her head. 'I also need posters to announce the events.'

'Print machine is broken,' the man droned.

'How long have you been the manager here?' Pru asked.

'Since yesterday,' he told her. 'I was a blacksmith in another town, but I got fired. I never had the right tools, the fire was never hot enough, and I forgot to order things. I was really lucky to get this job!'

'Yep. You sure were lucky,' Pru replied. That explained a lot. 'I need to make some changes to my plans,' she mused. 'I'll come back.'

'I'll be here,' he said, taking out a

cloth to wipe the countertop. 'Unless I get fired again.'

'I can't imagine why that would happen,' Pru muttered, but she didn't mean it.

She decided to go see Mr Winthrop about some ice cream. At first she considered having ice cream instead of lunch – kids loved that – but then she thought her father would be mad. She'd have to come up with a different lunch plan. Ice cream was for dessert.

'Mr Winthrop?' She called the owner's name as she entered the parlour. 'Where are you?'

'Pru!' he greeted. 'Nice to see you.' He stood behind the counter, but Pru noticed he wasn't wearing an apron.

'I need to order ice cream cones for the rodeo that starts tomorrow. Can you deliver them in the afternoon to the barn?'

'No can do,' Mr Winthrop said. 'I don't have cones. You see, they come from the bakery and the bakery doesn't have any flour.'

'I'm getting the feeling that the shipment didn't arrive because they ordered it from the supermarket.' Pru bit her bottom lip. 'You'll have cones on Friday?'

'How did you know?' His eyes went wide.

'Just a guess,' Pru said. She left the shop, feeling disappointed.

Chica Linda was waiting in the town square. Usually, seeing her horse cheered Pru up when she was feeling down, but not this time.

Pru said, 'Chica Linda, we are hitting rocks.' At the horse's confused look, Pru said, 'That means we aren't making any progress.'

Chica Linda chuffed and nuzzled her nose in Pru's hair.

'Thanks for the sympathy,' Pru said, giving her horse's nose a good scratch. 'But the families are coming tomorrow for the Wranglers' meeting and I have nothing for them to eat.' She opened her empty hands. 'Not a thing.'

Pru had promised her dad that she had everything under control, but now so many things were going wrong that she didn't know what to do.

'I can't have a rodeo without lunch or trophies or barrels,' she told Chica Linda. Yeah, she still hadn't solved the problem of what the horses would race around, since Turo was gone and there were no wooden barrels. Pretty much everything on her list was a bust.

'What are we going to do?' She was about to climb up into Chica Linda's saddle for a

quick ride – that usually cleared her head
– when Maricela came running up with a
letter in her hand.

'Pru!'

'Hey, Maricela,' she said, turning away
from Chica Linda. 'What's going on?'

'This letter was delivered to my house by
accident. I came to bring it to you,' Maricela
said.

'Thanks.' She took the letter.

'Is it from Abigail?' Maricela wanted
to know. 'Is she having a nice time at her
cousins' house? Is she talking about music?'
She looked at the letter in Pru's hand. 'She
asked me to teach her some music words
before she left so she would sound smarter
when she talked to her cousin.' Maricela
grinned. 'Did she use the words *octave* and
syncopation?'

'I haven't opened the letter yet,' Pru told Maricela.

'Well, do so,' Maricela said, putting her hands on her hips. 'I'll wait.'

Pru tore the seal on the envelope and took out the page.

'So? Did she talk about chord progression like I told her to?'

'I haven't read it,' Pru said. She scanned the letter quickly. 'Nothing about music,' Pru told Maricela.

'*Hmph,*' Maricela grunted. 'She'll never be fully accepted by her fancy cousin now. It's probably too late.' She rotated on her heel and began to walk away. 'I'll just go practise the song my vocal coach assigned.' Maricela turned back towards Pru. 'Unless you need anything.'

There was a hint of boredom in Maricela's

voice, and Pru wondered if maybe she was
trying to say she wanted to hang out longer.

Unless she had hot dog buns in her pantry
and maybe some trophies, Pru couldn't think
of a reason for Maricela to hang around. 'I
don't need anything. Thanks for the letter.'

Looking slightly disappointed, Maricela
said, 'Yeah. See ya.' She headed off towards
home.

Pru took Abigail's letter with her when she
climbed onto Chica Linda's saddle. She read
as she rode, and by the time she reached the
letter's end, Pru felt more confident that she
could solve the problems she'd encountered.
If Abigail could stay focused on being fancy,
Pru would stay focused on making the best
rodeo the wrangler kids had ever seen.

The challenge was on!

Dear Abigail,

I've been really upbeat and positive until now.

I hate to ask, but I have this really big favour. I mean, I really can't stand admitting this, but I hope you'll understand. I know you're with your cousins and how excited you were for the trip, but, with the way things are going, I think I need to ask both you and Lucky something important.

Can you come back?

I need you in Miradero.

You see, the kids are already here, and they are busy settling their horses into the stalls at the barn. They'll put out hay and water and set their saddles in the tack room.

Then, I'll gather them in a circle under the big shady tree.

And then ...

I've got nothing.

So not only do I need you to come back, but is there an outpost you could stop by for hot dog buns and trophies? If you could get ice cream cones, too, that would be helpful.

I'm desperate.

I thought I could do this by myself, but it turns out ... I can't. I need the PALs to make it all successful.

Oh, Abigail, I am in so much trouble. My dad keeps popping his head in and asking how things are going.

I tell him, 'Great,' because right now, everything _is_ great. And it's all gonna be great for about the next fifteen minutes until everyone realises that I've got nothing planned for the entire day. Or the next day. Or the day after that. And what am I going to do when the kids get hungry?

Did I mention there are fifteen kids? Not eight like my dad thought. Not even the ten he guessed would be the maximum. Fifteen!!!! And just one me!

Please, _please_ take Boomerang and hurry over here. You need to arrive in the next three or four minutes with all the supplies I listed above.

OK? Got it? Are you on your way yet?

<u>Sigh.</u> Of course you're not, because I'm still holding this letter. Even if I wasn't holding it and even if it was on its way and even if you could somehow be reading it instantly, there'd be no way for you to just immediately be here. I wish you <u>were</u> here, though.

The kids are pretty much done in the barn, and I think I hear tummies rumbling.

What am I going to do?!

Got to go. Hope to see you very, very soon.

PALs forever, unless my dad grounds me for life,

Pru

CHAPTER 7

Abigail put on her fanciest dress. She combed her hair and then curled the ends by wetting them and twisting them. After that, she put on her nice shoes and headed downstairs for breakfast.

She stopped by the large mirror in the hall to make sure she didn't have stray hay in her hair or dirt on her dress. Stuff like that happened all the time in Miradero, but she refused to let it happen here. Assuring herself that all was in order, she entered the breakfast room.

The long table was set for the whole family, but only her aunt and uncle were sitting there. Ashton was sleeping in a crib by the wall. Snips and Ariella hadn't arrived yet. Abigail assumed that was because Snips was getting dressed in his fine clothing as well. She'd told him to look his best today before they went to bed last night. He'd protested, but she'd insisted. And bribed him with ice cream later, so she knew he'd be wearing his clean trousers and a jacket whenever he came to breakfast. She probably should have reminded him of the time, but seeing as Snips was always hungry, she'd made the mistake of thinking he'd already be at the table.

'Good morning.' She greeted her aunt and uncle.

Uncle Tony peeked out over the newspaper he was reading. 'Ah, good day to you, Abigail.'

'Would you like some tea? Orange juice?'
Aunt Karen motioned for a server to bring
Abigail whatever she'd like. 'We can get you
hot chocolate, if you'd prefer.'

As delicious as that sounded, Lucky's
aunt had warned Abigail not to eat or drink
anything that might spill on her dress. So she
said, 'I'll have water,' even though that wasn't
what she wanted.

The glass of water appeared instantaneously,
as well as a plate of steaming-hot eggs and
toast. Jam was already on the table, but Abigail
avoided it because it was purple, and spilled
purple spots would clash with the pale-yellow
lace of her dress.

Being fancy was hard. Abigail was giving
up so many of the things she loved just to
make sure she fit in.

She glanced out the big picture window,

where she could see Boomerang in the distance. It was a good morning for a ride, but she couldn't go because that would mean changing clothes, and it was too hard to get out of the dress, plus she didn't want to mess up her hair.

'What are you doing today?' Uncle Tony asked as Abigail took a tiny bite of her eggs.

Before she answered, she looked at the doorway, hoping Snips and Ariella would appear. What use was being fancy if Ariella didn't see her?! She didn't need to prove herself to her aunt and uncle as much as to her cousin.

'I'm not sure,' Abigail said, returning her attention to her eggs.

'Ariella and Snips are down by the barn,' Aunt Karen said. 'Maybe after you eat, you could join them and see what they are up to.' She chuckled. 'I'm sure it's more fun than hanging out with us all day.' With that, Ashton started crying. Aunt Karen gathered him up and bounced him on her knee, cooing, 'Ashton, my love. I bet you want to go see what those big kids are doing, don't you?' She shook her head. 'You just need to grow a little first, and maybe learn to walk more than a few steps at a time.'

Uncle Tony laughed as if that were the funniest thing he'd ever heard. 'Learn to walk!' He slapped the table. 'That's a good one!'

While they carried on, not paying her any attention, Abigail shovelled huge forkfuls of eggs into her mouth and stuffed a whole piece of toast in after. She chewed. Gulped.

'Wow!' Uncle Tony remarked, noticing Abigail's clean plate. 'You must have been starving.'

Abigail smiled and gently dabbed the

corners of her mouth with her napkin.

'Thank you for a delicious breakfast.' She stood. 'I'll go now to meet my brother and cousin at the barn.' She punctuated that with a small curtsy, which was probably unnecessary, but after sneakily eating like a pig, she wanted them to see her as polite.

'Not the new barn,' Aunt Karen told her while giving a tiny bit of toast to Ashton. 'The old one.'

'I didn't know there was an old barn,' Abigail said, intrigued.

Uncle Tony told her where to go. It was a bit of a distance away, and she'd need to ride Boomerang. 'You might want to change your dress to something that can get dirty,' he suggested.

'I'm OK,' she replied. 'I'll be careful.' She really wanted Ariella to see her all

dressed up. 'I'll ride sidesaddle.' That way
she wouldn't risk wadding up her dress
and wrinkling it. Sidesaddle, Lucky's aunt
had told her, was the proper way that
gentlewomen rode.

'Have fun,' Aunt Karen said.

Abigail thanked her again, curtsied again,
and then slowly walked from the room. Once
out of sight of the adults, she took off running
towards the front door, then across the pasture
to get Boomerang ready for a ride.

The old barn was run-down, dusty and smelled
like mold. Abigail peeked her head inside to
find Snips standing there, looking down on a
box with wheels.

'Hey,' she said, careful to step over a wet

mud puddle in her nice shoes. 'What's going on?'

'We're building a soapbox race car,' Snips said proudly, holding up a screwdriver. 'There's a derby this weekend, and Ariella said I could drive.'

Of all the things in the world that they could be doing, this was the one Abigail least expected.

Ariella crawled out from under a wooden board that was sitting on bricks. She was wearing jeans that had been cut off at the knees and what looked like an old shirt of her dad's. Snips was wearing the outfit that Abigail had told him to put on, only it was covered with mud and dirt and ... was that a jam stain from breakfast?

Lucky's aunt would be so ashamed.

'A soapbox ... what?' Abigail asked, stepping inside the barn and closing the door behind her.

'A soapbox race car,' Ariella said simply.

'A soapbox works with gravy,' Snips explained. 'That means no motor.'

96

'Gravity,' Abigail corrected. 'It's the way the earth naturally pulls things towards each other.'

'Gravy,' Snips repeated. 'Yep. Just like gravy moves towards the potatoes, this car is going to move to the finish line.' He grinned. 'Only faster.'

Ariella wiped her hands on her trouser legs. 'As Snips said, there's a derby this weekend, so we have to build a car for it. You can help ... if you want.' She looked pointedly at Abigail's dress.

Abigail wasn't sure what to do or say. Ariella had invited her to help but not at first. She'd gone off with Snips without telling her. Then again, this was way better than fancy-prancing around the house all day and trying not to get dirty. 'Um ... yeah, of course I can help!'

Ariella shrugged. 'There's another

screwdriver over in the toolbox.' She pointed at a metal box by Snips's foot. 'We're going to need some lug bolts, a few fender washers, and another piece of wood. You can cut wood, can't you?'

Looking around at their setup, Abigail reached over and picked up a handsaw. 'Yup. What size boards do you need?'

'Fourteen by fourteen inches for the seat,' Ariella replied. 'You sure you don't want to change clothes first?'

'I'm good,' Abigail said, gripping the saw. She didn't want to return to the house and then come back. They might be done by then, and she'd miss the fun if she left. A little dirt in her hair or on her dress wouldn't hurt.

Abigail took up the saw and began to cut the board for the base of the car.

'I think if Snips is driving, we might want to make everything a little smaller,' she suggested.

'I want it bigger!' Snips protested.

'Make it fifteen by fifteen, then,' Ariella told Abigail.

'I really think –'

'Bigger!' Snips insisted, and Ariella agreed.

'If you say so.' Abigail cut the board, then held it up next to Snips. 'You're going to slide all over this seat.'

'Sliding is fun,' Snips said, and Ariella agreed again.

Next, Abigail began work on the front axle. 'We could measure how long Snips's arms are,' she suggested. 'So he can reach the brake easily.'

'I have gorilla arms,' Snips said. *'Oooh, oooh, oooh!'* He bounced around the barn, splashing in the mud puddle and spraying mud

99

speckles on Abigail's dress. 'Make the brake shorter, Abigail. My arms will reach!'

'I don't think they will,' Abigail said, desperately trying to scrape the mud off her dress but smearing it instead. 'I guess we can make the steering rope longer.'

'Nope!' Snips protested. 'I'll lean forward like this.' He showed her how he'd bend over to reach the steering rope. 'I'm going to be the fastest driver on the course. Let the gravy take me to victory!'

'Gravity,' Abigail corrected again.

'Victory!' Ariella cheered. 'We love victory! Abigail, don't adjust the rope or the seat or the brakes,' Ariella told her. 'We'll do it Snips's way!'

'He's never driven a soapbox before,' Abigail said, feeling exasperated. 'He's going to get hurt if we don't make adjustments.' She'd never driven a soapbox before, either, but changing things for Snips's size made sense.

'The bigger the car, the faster I'll go,' Snips said. 'Maybe I can get Señor Carrots to give me a push at the beginning. He's got a lotta muscle and could make me go even faster.' Snips thought about it and told Abigail, 'Hold your ponies! I'm a genius! I think we should make the seat big enough for Señor Carrots to ride with me. He could be my assistant. Maybe we could even tie the steering ropes around his ears and teach him to use the brake pedals.'

'That would be amazing!' Ariella exclaimed. 'We could be the first cart in history to be driven by a donkey! The whole town would be so impressed.'

'Maybe after we win the race, we could be in the newspaper,' Snips said. 'Everyone who has a donkey would be so jealous.'

'Yes!' Ariella cheered. 'And all we have to

do is to make sure the seat is big enough for both you and Señor Carrots.'

'Or I could sit *on* Señor Carrots, and he could stand on the seat,' Snips suggested.

Abigail stared, jaw open, eyes wide, at her cousin and brother.

Were they serious?

'What do you think, Abigail?' Ariella asked. But then before she could answer, she told Snips, 'We're going to need a longer steering rope.'

'Are you even allowed to have more than one person driving?' Abigail asked.

'Not more than one *person*!' Snips told her, and Ariella nodded in agreement. 'Donkeys aren't people, so we'll be perfectly fine.'

If the two of them had stopped talking for a second, Abigail would have said that she felt uncertain about this donkey plan. It was dangerous for Snips to drive such a big car, and there was no way Señor Carrots was going to agree to this scheme.

Abigail tried to find an opening to tell them they needed to listen to her and make a Snips-size soapbox. But Ariella and Snips were going on and on about how to rig the car to let his donkey drive.

Abigail eventually gave up. They weren't listening. They no longer needed her there. She slipped out the back of the old barn, unnoticed. Boomerang was waiting for her in the field.

'Let's go for a ride,' she said and, giving up any pretense of being fancy, she leaped on Boomerang's back, let her mud – and sawdust – covered skirt flop over the saddle in every direction, and rode off towards the hills at a gallop.

Dear Lucky,

It's derby day.
I know that doesn't mean
anything yet, but I'll explain. It
turns out that Ariella is _not_ fancy
at all. Her family is fancy and
their house is fancy and their life
is fancy, but if you scratch off the
fancy, Ariella is ... well, whatever the
opposite of fancy is.

Had I known that she wasn't
what I expected, I'd never have
taken manners lessons with your
aunt. I'd have brought more

comfortable clothing and shoes that didn't pinch my toes until they turned blue like crumpled little blueberries.

Anyhoo, apparently Ariella and Snips have been off together building a soapbox race car. Now I may not know anything about soapbox race cars, but I know that their car is never going to work. It's just too big for Snips _or_ Ariella! Snips got it into his head that Señor Carrots should drive the car with him, but I don't know how that's supposed to work. I told them a million times that Señor Carrots would never sit in the car, and a seat that is big enough for a donkey would be way too big for either of them. But would he listen? No. Would Ariella listen? No. They were too busy figuring out how to make it so Señor Carrots could ride in the soapbox car <u>with</u> Snips.

And guess what? Call me 'Surprised.' OK, don't really call me that, but I am surprised.

That lazy donkey loves riding in the car. So far, they've only slowly pulled him around the old barn, but the plan is for him to ride the racetrack with Snips. It's ridiculous! I think Señor Carrots thinks he's just going to be pulled around, having fun — not flying down a hill faster than a shooting star.

Sometimes I think I am making things up, but I am not. This story seems too fake to be true. So, here's what I need you to do. Squint your eyes and look in my direction. Can you see Snips at the starting line in a soapbox racer that is as big as a ... donkey? I see him.

If you can see what I see, then you'll see that Ariella is trying to lead Señor Carrots onto the platform with a lead rope. The donkey's being stubborn. Maybe he's figured out their real plan? Or maybe he's just being himself. I can't tell from here.

Boomerang and I want nothing to do with this nonsense. We rode out to a hill where we can see but not hear. It's better for us to be far, far away so I can ignore Ariella and Snips not listening to me.

Snips told me they're going to do a practise run before the real race, just to get Señor Carrots used to the hill.

At any rate, they were finally able to get Señor Carrots in the car.

Snips clambered on top of him and is holding steering ropes attached to the wheel. He's talking for a minute with Ariella and is now turning back to the hill. Ariella is giving the car a shove and ...

There they go.

The donkey is driving better than I thought. They made the first right turn without a problem. Señor Carrots's foot is tied to the brake. Snips is shouting (yes, I can hear him – he's loud). He's telling the donkey to pull the brake as they go into the next curve.

Señor Carrots is not pulling the brake.

Snips is yelling louder.

Ariella is running alongside the track, and now she's yelling, too.

I'm really far away and even <u>I'm</u> yelling.

It doesn't look like Ariella or Snips taught Señor Carrots how to pull the brake pedal.

So now, instead of turning around the next curve, Snips and Señor Carrots are going too fast and are going right off the racetrack! They're racing across the grass — I can see Snips bouncing up and down from all the little bumps in the ground. And ... and ...

They've barrelled right into a huge bunch of bushes!
Oh no!

PALs forever and ever,

Abigail ✿

CHAPTER 8

L ucky took Spirit out for a ride.

She had to get away and figure out what to do. She could protest her family moving away from Miradero, but she didn't think that would do her any good. It was extra hard because her dad and Kate seemed so happy in Destiny Falls.

Kate came back from her tour of the school all excited about the programmes they were running and the new books and new desks and all the things they had here that Miradero didn't have. Her dad gushed on and on about the good restaurants and the fancy train station plans. It was going to be an example to the entire frontier of what could be built!

Lucky sighed and gave Spirit a nudge to gallop faster. She needed some real speed if she was going to figure out a plan.

'Lucky!' Spirit was about to round a bend in the path when Lucky heard her name called. 'Slow down!'

A horse came galloping behind her. She slowed to let the rider catch up, then instantly regretted her decision.

'Julian ... ' Lucky groaned. '*Why* are you still following me?'

'You owe me a pound from last night,' he said with a grin. 'I came to collect.' Her cousin held out his hand.

'I bet you a pound you couldn't eat all the popcorn you bought at the theatre.'

'And I ate it,' Julian said. 'Some last night,

a handful for breakfast, and the rest today for lunch.' He pulled the empty container from his back pocket. 'It was delicious. Pound, please.'

'You're ... ' What was the word Aunt Cora sometimes used to mean *annoying in a big way*? 'Insufferable.'

'If by *insufferable* you mean *delightful*,' Julian said smugly.

Not wanting to argue, and hoping to get away for the rest of her ride, Lucky gave over one of the pounds her dad had given her.

'For another pound, I'll tell you something you don't know.' Julian already had his hand out to be paid.

'Just tell me,' Lucky said.

'Pound first.'

It was the last of the five. One by one, he'd managed to get them all. This was meant to be the pound Lucky had bet him that he couldn't make her like Destiny Falls. The truth was, she really did like it here; she just didn't want to move from Miradero. She'd never tell him that, and she was determined to protect her last pound from his pocket.

'No,' Lucky said, starting to move down the path with Spirit, hoping that Julian would get the hint.

'But I have my eye on a book at the bookshop,' Julian said.

While it was amazing that the town had an actual bookshop where you could get the books you wanted whenever you wanted them, Lucky would rather order them from the Miradero library and wait for the books to arrive, no matter how long it took.

'You don't read,' Lucky said. 'I bet you don't even know how.'

Julian snorted. 'I read a book once. I liked it. I just never have time to read.'

'Because you're too busy thinking about ideas to snake money,' Lucky said. 'Now if you'll excuse me.' Spirit moved into a gallop. Julian struggled to keep up.

'Then you don't want to know that you're ... moving here?' he shouted as the distance between them grew.

The idle word – the most important word – was muddled. Spirit skidded to a stop, and Julian and his horse ricocheted past. They stopped then turned to come back.

'My pound,' Julian said. 'I told you the information, now you cough it up.'

'No way.' Lucky stared at him. 'What did you just say?'

'Without that pound, I can assure you that I said nothing.' Julian spurred his horse to go back into town.

'Fine!' Lucky had to know that she'd heard him correctly. 'I'll give you the pound.'

'You *aren't* moving here.' Julian smiled and pocketed the pound.

'Wait, *what*?' Lucky pulled Spirit up closer to Julian. 'What do you *mean* I'm not moving here?'

'Just what I said,' he replied with a shrug.

'But how do you know?'

'Because for *some* reason, Aunt Kate and Uncle Jim love that rinky-dink town of Miradero as much as you do.' Julian rolled his eyes.

'B-but the school and the railroad meetings,' Lucky spluttered. 'And what about the barn and those new friends and the house next to yours?'

'Aunt Kate was just trying to get ideas for how to make your school better, Uncle Jim was telling everyone about all the work he did in Miradero, I showed you that barn to actually see how Spirit liked it, my friends were to show you how great Destiny Falls is, and I told you about the house because ... ' Julian trailed off.

'Because?' Lucky prompted him. She could feel her patience growing thin. 'Because why?'

Julian huffed. 'Because ... well ... maybe if you liked Destiny Falls ... maybe you would move here, too!' He wrinkled his nose.

'Move here, too?' Lucky was shocked.

'Well, yeah,' Julian said, looking away. 'We always have fun together, don't we? It might be more fun if you actually lived here.'

Lucky frowned. 'Destiny Falls is nice ... really nice ... and I have had fun here, at least when I wasn't worried about moving, but Miradero is my home. It's where my friends live and where Spirit lives. I couldn't leave there.' Julian looked disheartened. 'But,' Lucky continued, 'that doesn't mean that I can't come and visit. Destiny Falls isn't that far from Miradero. And I'm sure that my dad will want to come here more often to see how the railroad is going. We could have more … fun.'

Julian looked up at her and his face broke into his signature grin. 'Yeah … maybe you're right. Plus, I could even visit Miradero more and run that town next.' As Lucky started to protest, he laughed. 'Now if you don't mind, I've got a book to buy.' He shook the pound coin at her. 'See ya, RF.' In a flash, he was gone.

Lucky could have easily caught up with him and his horse, but she had something bigger that she had to do. She wasn't moving! That was the important part. But she'd sent the letter to Pru that very morning, asking her and Abigail to cut their holidays short to come to town to help her convince her dad to stay in Miradero!

'Spirit,' Lucky told her trusty steed, 'I am going to choose to believe that Julian wasn't tricking us this time. And if he wasn't tricking us, then we have to stop the mail so we don't ruin anyone else's holidays!'

Lucky and Spirit galloped down the path back towards town, dodging slow-moving riders and carriages and cutting through trees. As they reached the main post office, Lucky leaped off Spirit, immediately broke into a sprint, and burst her way through the front doors.

The man at the desk looked up in alarm at the sudden interruption. 'Can I help you, miss?'

Lucky was breathing deeply. 'Hi, I'm so sorry to bother you, but has the mail carrier left for the day? It's really, really, *really* important.'

The man frowned. 'You just missed her.

She left a few minutes ago to head to the next town!'

'Oh no!' Lucky turned on her heel and headed towards the door. 'Thank you!' she called as she dashed outside.

Lucky thought quickly as she swung onto Spirit's back. If the carrier had left only a few minutes ago, Lucky might still be able to catch her before she got too far away! Lucky nudged Spirit's sides with her heels and took off down the main road out of town. The buildings became fewer and further between, and the people and horses became more sparse. Lucky followed the railroad tracks for guidance, heading the opposite way from how she, her dad and Kate had come only days before.

Just as Lucky was ready to give up and turn around, upset that she may have scared her friends and ruined their holidays for no good reason, she saw the speck of a horse and its rider up ahead.

She bent low over Spirit's neck. 'Just a little further, Spirit,' she whispered. Spirit shot forward and, within moments, had pulled up next to the horse and its rider. It was the mail carrier!

Lucky waved wildly at her to slow down, and the woman pulled on her horse's reins in confusion. Lucky and Spirit also slowed until the two horses were at a standstill.

'Whoa there,' the carrier said. 'Is everything all right?'

'No! I mean, yes, everything is fine now, but that actually makes it *not* all right,' Lucky said in a rush.

The mail carrier's brow furrowed. 'I'm sorry, I don't quite understand.'

Lucky took a moment to gather herself.

'Well,' she explained, 'my cousin made me think we were moving away from Miradero to Destiny Falls, and I don't *want* to move away from Miradero because I *love* it there, so I sent a letter to my friends asking them to cut their holidays short and come help me convince my dad not to move, but it turns out we're *not* actually moving, so my friends don't need to come and help me.'

'Oh.' The carrier somehow looked more confused than before.

'So,' Lucky continued slowly, 'if you don't mind, I really need that letter back that I sent this morning because I don't want them to get the letter and ruin their holidays.'

'*Hmm.* I see.' The carrier pressed her lips together.

'So ... can I have the letter?'

The carrier shook her head. 'I'm afraid

not, miss. I'm sorry, but that letter has already been postmarked and is due to arrive at its destination. I can't just let you take it.'

Lucky frowned. 'OK, well, can I write a new letter to go along with it?'

The carrier shook her head again. 'I'm sorry, but mail needs to go through the post office before I take it,' she said.

'Oh, please,' Lucky said, 'if my friends, the PALs, think I'm in trouble, they'll worry and ruin their weeks by coming to try and stop my dad. That would make everything messy because I just made a mistake. I really want them to keep having fun and not spend their time worrying about something that's not even happening.'

'Hmmm ...' The woman looked up and down the empty street. 'I still have to deliver the mail, but I don't think there's a rule about

you changing the letter. Think you can do that instead of just taking it back?'

'Oh, that's a great idea!' Lucky cheered. 'I definitely think I can do that, no problem.'

'Don't write a whole new letter,' the carrier said. 'Just cross out the parts that are wrong.' The woman dug Lucky's letter out of her bag and gave Lucky a pencil.

Lucky opened the envelope carefully so it could be resealed. Then she started making changes.

Dear Pru,

~~I think something terrible is~~
~~happening. I haven't been able to~~
~~talk to my dad about it yet because~~
~~I can't seem to get him alone, but ...~~
~~I think we're moving to Destiny Falls!~~
~~Julian has been showing me around~~
~~the town all day, and he keeps saying~~
~~how much I'd like the school and how~~
~~much Spirit will like the stables and~~
~~how the house right next to his is for~~
~~sale. Julian certainly seems sure that~~
~~we're moving, and I can't help thinking~~
~~he's right!~~

Julian and I went to see a show
tonight. The play itself was amazing.
There were bright lights and really
beautiful costumes, and the story was

about a group of three friends — just like us! It would've been a night out of a dream, except for the sound of Julian crunching on popcorn next to me the entire time. Afterwards, my dad was supposed to meet us at the ice cream parlour. ~~I was going to try again to talk to him about the move,~~ but he never showed up!

Apparently, he didn't make his dinner date with Kate, either. My dad was still at a meeting with the railroad people until late, and when I got home, Kate was asleep. So I just went to sleep, too. He must have been out most of the night.

~~I know, I know. I shouldn't jump to conclusions without asking someone about it, but it's as if Dad and Kate~~

~~aren't even on this holiday with~~
~~me! Here, let me tell you what I know.~~
~~I'm sure if you reason it out how~~
~~Boxcar Bonnie does, you'll agree that~~
~~all signs point to us moving to Destiny~~
~~Falls.~~

1. Julian showed Spirit the
    amazing local barn and bet me
    how much Spirit would like it.
    (It _is_ really nice but definitely
    not as nice as yours.)

2. Dad told Julian to introduce
    me to people so I could make
    new friends. ~~(He said —~~
    ~~actually said — it would be~~
    ~~good for me to make new~~
    ~~friends, as if I needed to~~
    ~~replace the friends I already~~
    ~~have!)~~

3. Kate is meeting with the school principal today. (~~Why would she need to meet with the principal here unless it was for a job?~~)

4. Kate brought pretty much everything she owned on this holiday. (~~I wish I'd never joked about us moving here.~~)

5. The house next to Julian's is for sale and my dad told me to go see it with him. (~~Why would I need to go see some silly house?!~~)

6. My dad is in important meetings all day every day. (~~It's like they can't make any decisions without him.~~)

7. Dad keeps asking if I like it here. (~~As if he really cares!~~)

That's seven clues. That's more clues than even Boxcar Bonnie ever uses. She only needs three or four clues, and then she's certain enough to solve the mystery. I don't need to talk to my dad anymore because my clues can only point to one thing.

We're moving to Destiny Falls.

Pru! Help! I need to do something before everything gets settled!

I need to convince my dad that we can't — just CAN'T — move away from Miradero, but I'm not going to be able to do it alone. I need you and Abigail to drop what you're doing and come here right now to help me convince my dad not to make us move so no one buys a new house or gets a new job or anything like that! I know you have

the rodeo and that Abigail is having
fun with her family, but you need to
go get her and then hurry to Destiny
Falls — before it's too late.

          —

PALs forever?

    Lucky ☆

'Whew,' Lucky said. The letter didn't make a ton of sense, but it was much better than before, and no one would worry if they read it. She put the letter back in the envelope and gave it to the mail carrier. 'Thanks again.'

The woman smiled as she tucked the letter back in her bag. 'You're welcome. It sounds like you've got a great group of friends.' With a click of her tongue, she and her horse continued on in the direction of Miradero.

Giving a happy sigh of relief, Lucky turned Spirit around and hurried back to Destiny Falls.

Hopefully, her dad and Kate would want to go out for dinner soon. All that riding had left Lucky starving.

CHAPTER 9

'I want to race!' Snips was sitting on the ground next to the bushes, pulling twigs out of his hair as Abigail fussed over him.

'That is *not* happening,' Abigail declared. She looked over to where Señor Carrots was busy munching on the hedge that the car had crashed into. The donkey didn't have a scratch on him. Snips, on the other hand, had scrapes and scratches all over his arms, legs, and, oddly, the back of his neck. The good news was, by the way he was arguing with her, Abigail could tell nothing was broken.

'But, Abigail,' Snips whined, 'we spent

all week preparing for this.' He looked over at Ariella for support, but she was busy extracting the car from the shrub.

'You can't possibly be serious,' Abigail told him, sounding very motherly. 'Your soapbox-car days are over.'

'Ugh, come *on*, Abigail.'

'No,' she said firmly.

Snips crossed his arms and scrunched up his face in a pout. 'Ariella knew you wouldn't understand.'

Abigail stood up straight in surprise and glanced over to Ariella, who had frozen as she tugged the soapbox car onto the grass. 'What do you mean, I wouldn't understand?' She looked at Snips, but he just stared at the ground, knowing he had slipped up. She looked back at Ariella. 'Well?'

Ariella shuffled her feet, refusing to make eye contact with Abigail. 'Well ... it just seemed like soapbox racing wouldn't really be your … thing.'

Abigail frowned. 'But why not?'

Ariella looked up at her. 'You're just so … *fancy*! You would never want to be dirty and build things!' she exclaimed.

'Me? Fancy?' Abigail was shocked.

'Yes!' Ariella said. 'I mean, I used to think you were so interesting and we had so much fun doing those bonfires and stuff, but now you wear those nice clothes and curtsy and talk all funny!'

'But I thought *you* were fancy! You said exploring is boring!' Abigail protested.

'Exploring *is* boring when you've lived in the same place your entire life,' Ariella said stubbornly.

Abigail sighed. 'Fine, you have a point there. But honestly, I was just trying to be fancy because I thought I would fit in better with you. I wanted to spend time with you, but it felt like you only wanted to spend time with Snips. I still love riding my horse and having bonfires and getting messy! Those shoes hurt my toes!'

Ariella giggled, but then got serious again. 'I'm sorry,' she said. 'I figured you wouldn't be interested in building a car with us. I should have asked you instead of assuming.'

Abigail smiled. 'I'm sorry, too. I should have just been myself! If I could do this whole week over, I would. And I would bring more trousers!'

'I would, too,' Ariella agreed, 'especially since the car doesn't matter much now.'

'What do you mean?'

'We made it too big! If Snips is too short for it, then I'm *definitely* too short to drive it.' Ariella gestured at her small frame.

'*Hmm.*' Abigail tapped on her chin. 'What if ... I drove it instead?'

'You?!' Snips said from the ground.

Abigail nodded down at him. 'I'm much taller than either of you. I won't slide around as much in the seat, and I'll probably be able to reach the brake.'

Ariella's face lit up in a smile. 'That would be amazing!'

Abigail clapped her hands happily. 'Then it's settled! Let's get this race car ready.'

Snips scrambled to his feet. Together, the three of them grabbed the end and tugged it out of the bushes. After a couple of tries, they were able to get it out of the branches. They excitedly circled the car, checking it for damage.

'It all looks OK,' Snips said. 'I guess Señor Carrots and I weren't such bad drivers after all!'

'I wouldn't be so sure about that,' Ariella said glumly. She was crouching next to one of the back wheels. Abigail and Snips hurried to Ariella's side and looked over her shoulders.

'What's wrong?' Abigail asked.

'Is it broken?' Snips worried.

Abigail pointed to the axle that held the wheel. 'Look, a part of the axle is damaged. The wheel isn't secure anymore.' Abigail looked closely and saw there was a small gap between the wheel and the axle where a piece of wood had chipped off from the impact. 'If we don't fill that gap, the wheel might not stay on and there might be an even worse crash,' Ariella finished.

Abigail took a step back to think. They needed something narrow enough to fit in the gap that would be flexible enough to move with the wheel. Suddenly it came to her.

'My letter!' she cried, reaching into her back pocket.

Snips and Ariella looked back at her in confusion. 'Your letter?'

Hurriedly, Abigail folded and twisted the letter. She reached past her brother and her cousin and fit the paper into the gap. '*Mm-hmm*. I wrote a letter earlier to one of my friends, but I don't need to send it now. That should hold until the end.'

The three pushed the car back and forth a bit to make sure the wheel would hold. When everything looked good, Abigail grinned. 'Let's show off what our family can do … together!'

Suddenly, there was an announcement for all racers to report to the starting line. Together, Abigail, Ariella and Snips pushed the car back up the hill with all the other cars. Abigail carefully climbed into the race car. The seat fit her just fine. She checked that she was able to reach the brake and the steering. They were both perfect. She gave a thumbs-up to her cousin and her brother on the sidelines. They gave thumbs-ups back.

There was a countdown from three.

Then the man with the flag shouted, 'Go!' He swung the flag down in a mighty arc.

'Wahoo!' Abigail shouted as the soapbox race car flew down the hill.

CHAPTER 10

'Pru.' Mrs Prescott called her name from the front of the class. 'How about if you go first today and tell us about your half term?'

'I have to go first?' Pru moaned. 'Can't Lucky go first?'

'I'll go first!' Snips exclaimed, holding up his first-place soapbox derby trophy. 'I'm the King of First!' He hadn't stopped bragging about the trophy from the minute Abigail had crossed the finish line in the race. Abigail let him have the trophy with the agreement that they'd take turns with it and he'd bring it back for Ariella next time they visited.

Snips carried the gold cup everywhere
he went.

'I think we all heard about that race. You
made a tour of the town, stopping at nearly
every house,' Mrs Prescott said.

'*Every* house,' Snips assured her. 'When
we got back from our cousins' house, Señor
Carrots and I threw our own victory parade.'
He frowned. 'But no one showed up, so that's
why we knocked on doors. *Everyone* needed
to know the news!' He raised the trophy.
'First-place winner. That's me. I couldn't
have done it without the help of my cousin
Ariella.'

Abigail sighed. 'And?' she said expectantly.

'And my sister, I guess.' Snips rolled his
eyes.

Mrs Prescott nodded wearily. 'Once again,
I say for us all, congratulations.'

Snips stood. 'Time for my presentation to the class.'

Mrs Prescott quickly wrote Snips's name on the chalkboard and drew a check mark next to it. 'I think we can all agree, Snips, that you've more than given us your presentation already.'

'Pru.' Lucky leaned over from her seat. 'You'd be doing us all a big favour if you'd speak. I mean, I spent the whole holiday with our teacher, and Snips is going to start up again any second ...'

Pru leaped out of her chair. 'Fine, I'll do it. I'll go first.'

'Second,' Snips corrected, pointing at his name on the board and raising his trophy.

Pru sighed and moved up to the front of the class.

'So it turns out that my big job over break was to organise a children's rodeo. But when

143

it came down to it, the rodeo was not going well,' she began, pausing to consider how best to tell the tale. 'Mrs Prescott? I think I need some help telling what happened.'

'I don't understand, Pru,' Mrs Prescott said. 'It's your story.'

'Nah,' Pru said, then she pointed to her classmates. 'It's their story, too.'

Mrs Prescott tilted her head, confused. 'Go on …'

'I was in the barn with the fifteen rodeo kids! I had no lunch, no trophies, no barrels, no ice cream cones, no real plans whatsoever. It was a disaster. I thought I would be able to handle it all by myself, since my PALs were out of town, but luckily I had some other friends come to the rescue.' She pointed to Maricela, who stood and came to stand next to Pru.

'I brought lunch,' Maricela said proudly. 'I

mean, Cook prepared sandwiches and carried them, but I asked her to make them and I led the way.'

Pru turned to Maricela as if she were a reporter, getting the interview. 'And why did you do that?'

Maricela shrugged. 'I was bored. I'd painted three landscapes, learned four new songs to sing, and I noticed that Pru needed help.' She smiled. 'I needed something to write about for my speech.' She held up twenty pages.

'And I'm sure it's a wonderful speech. I can't wait to hear it,' Mrs Prescott assured Maricela.

Pru grinned. 'Lunch was delicious. And then … ' She pointed at Turo.

'I brought barrels.' He stood up and walked over to Pru as well. He told the class how he'd been worried about Pru ever since he'd told her he was leaving town. 'I came back, just in time.'

Mary Pat and Bianca stood at the same time. 'We helped, too!' they said together.

'We were walking by Snips's house,' Bianca said, batting her eyelashes.

'Ugh,' Mary Pat groaned.

'We'd been sick the whole holiday, and it was our first day outside,' Bianca said. 'I wanted to see if Snips was home yet. I made him brownies.'

Snips looked conflicted at the news. He liked brownies, but Bianca? Not so much.

'We heard the cheering from Pru's porch ... ' Mary Pat said.

'And decided to check it out,' Bianca continued.

'We provided the brownies for snacks and got to be the event judges,' Mary Pat said.

'And there was one other helper I couldn't

have done it without ...' Pru said with a grin. Suddenly there was a snort and a neigh from outside the schoolhouse window. The kids all ran to look out. Chica Linda was there with Boomerang and Spirit. Chica Linda whinnied.

'Chica Linda gave up some of the ribbons that she'd earned in old competitions so I could remake them into new ribbons for the kids at the rodeo!' Pru reached out the window to rub Chica Linda's nose. 'Real winners don't need trophies.'

'Yes, they do,' Snips said, hugging his trophy tightly.

Pru turned back to Mrs Prescott and said, 'I wrote letters to Abigail and Lucky begging them to come help me, but it turned out that all the help I needed was right here all along.' She smiled. Then quickly added, 'Though I wish that Lucky and Abigail had been there.'

'We wish we were there, too,' Abigail said.

'Well, since I'm not moving away,' Lucky said, 'maybe we can plan to host the Wranglers' meeting and kids' rodeo again next year?'

'I'll ask my dad ...' Pru started, but then realised what she'd heard. 'What do you mean you *aren't* moving away?'

Lucky winked at Kate and said, 'It was a big misunderstanding.'

Kate stepped in front of the room and said, 'Lucky, maybe you should tell the class about your holiday?'

Lucky considered what to say. 'Destiny Falls is a nice place to visit, but' – she wrapped her arms around her best friends – 'Miradero is my home.'

Read on for a sneak
peek at another
Spirit Riding Free
adventure in
Abigail's Diary ...

❀ Abigail's Diary ❀

I've never had a diary before, but thanks to Lucky and Pru, the best PALs ever, I do now. What a nice present! They said I should write down everything about the Frontier Fillies Summer Jubilee because I am so excited.

Wait, hang on a hot minute ... maybe they got me the diary so I'd stop talking to <u>them</u> about the Jubilee?

Oh, what am I even thinking? That can't be! That's impossible. Pru and Lucky love hearing me talk about the Jubilee and all the things we are going to do there.

I mean, who <u>wouldn't</u> want to talk about the Frontier Fillies Summer Jubilee?!

It's going to be the best Frontier Fillies event the frontier has ever seen. At the Summer Jubilee, everyone can earn pins with their horses!

It's gonna be three whole days of fun with other Frontier Fillies herds from all over. We're going to make friends and eat s'mores and giggle and <u>earn those pins!</u>

Join Abigail on the next adventure!